JAMES STEVENSON

NO LAUGHING, NO SMILING, NO GIGGLING

FRANCES FOSTER BOOKS
FARRAR, STRAUS AND GIROUX
NEW YORK

For Eugenie Sherer, with admiration

Copyright © 2004 by James Stevenson
All rights reserved
Distributed in Canada by Douglas & McIntyre Ltd.
Color separations by Chroma Graphics PTE Ltd.
Printed and bound in the United States of America by Berryville Graphics
Designed by Nancy Goldenberg
First edition, 2004
10 9 8 7 6 5 4 3 2 1

www.fsgkidsbooks.com

Library of Congress Cataloging-in-Publication Data
Stevenson, James, date.
  No laughing, no smiling, no giggling / James Stevenson.— 1st ed.
      p.   cm.
    Summary: The reader joins Freddy Fafnaffer the pig as he deals with Mr.
Frimdimpny, a crocodile who never laughs and who decides on the rules for reading
this book.
    ISBN 0-374-31829-8
    [1. Laughter—Fiction.   2. Behavior—Fiction.   3. Pigs—Fiction.   4. Crocodiles—
Fiction.]   I. Title.
PZ7.S84748Nof 2004
[E]—dc21
                                                                    2003045508

HOW TO READ THIS BOOK

Welcome to this book!
My name is Freddy
Fafnaffer and I am
the *nice* one.

The other person
is NOT so nice.
... In fact, he is not
nice at all.

Mr. Frimdimpny never laughs
or smiles or giggles . . .
and he HATES it when other
people do!
So he makes up rules . . .

Uh-oh . . . I hear his wet
slippery footsteps!
Mr. Frimdimpny is coming!

SHLOOP
SCOONCH
SHLOOP
SCOONCH

I am Mr. Frimdimpny!
I am in charge of this book!

H-he's in
ch-charge of
this b-book!

SHLOOP SCOONCH

You must do what *I* say!

Read the rules, Fafnaffer!

Y-yes, Mr. Frimdimpny.
Rule number 1 says:
Do not laugh
or smile
or giggle.

**And what
happens
if you laugh
or smile or giggle?**

You have
to go back
to the front
of the book!

Yes! Yes! Yes!

And what is rule number 2?

Rule number 2 says:
Do not do anything
you are told
NOT to do.

Or?

Or you have to go
all the way back
to the front of
the book!

THAT
WAY.

Is that understood?

IS IT? IS IT? IS IT?

Now I am going away for a moment . . .

NOBODY FOLLOW ME!

I have a secret. My secret is so secret I have to go far away just to tell myself what my secret is.

SCOONCH SHLOOP

Nobody can hear me out here . . .

Now you may start the book!

**. . . Fafnaffer!
I see you
SMILING!**

Me?

Go back to the front of the book!

Yes, Mr. Frimdimpny.

THE BEST-DRESSED MAN

Tonight is my big night!
I, Mr. Freshley Prest Panz, Jr.,
am about to get the prize
for best-dressed man in the world!

The crowd is
waiting—
are you ready,
Mr. Panz?

There . . . I am as perfectly dressed as a person can get.

Something is crawling inside my shirt!

And here he is, ladies and gentlemen—
the best-dressed man in the world!

**You did not smile,
did you?**

**If you did,
go back to
the front of
the book . . .**

YUCK!

THE WORLD'S TINIEST CIRCUS

Step right up . . .
A ticket is only ten cents!

Oops! I just
stepped on
an elephant!

I'm very sorry!
Are you all
right, sir?

Six . . .
seven . . .
eight . . .

It's showtime! Begin the parade! Here they come! Horses first, then the clowns, the acrobats, the jugglers, the elephants . . . What a circus!

I can't see them . . .

If you want to see the tiny creatures, you must turn the page VERY VERY SLOWLY. Otherwise they will blow away . . .

**You call that "slowly"?
You turned the page
too fast!**

The circus has blown away!
There goes a lion . . .
There go three clowns . . .

Go back to the front of the book!

Ten cents gone
and no circus . . .
Maybe it was
just a trick . . .

Look!
An enormous
magnifying glass!

I wonder what you can see?

Wow! A tiny circus!
It's definitely worth ten cents!

THE FANCY CONCERT

When you go to
a fancy concert,
NEVER take a
red balloon.

It could escape in the
middle of the fancy concert.

LISTEN CAREFULLY!
This is the red balloon you must NOT blow on!

If you do, the balloon
might float onto the
stage and interrupt the
fancy concert!
I will now turn my back.
I know you will not blow
on the balloon . . .

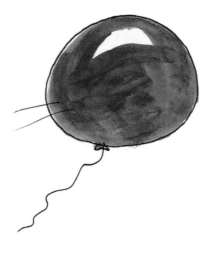

I told you NOT to blow on it!

Now it is floating toward the stage.

Ladies and gentlemen—
the fancy concert is over!

THE NICE NAP

I am tired out from telling people what not to do.

SCOONCH SHLOOP

I will spread my blankie and take a nice nap.

Why, Mr. Frimdimpny appears to be taking a nap!

You go first!

It's working!
He's giggling in his sleep!

Look out!
Mr. Frimdimpny is ROLLING OVER!

Now we're in big trouble . . .
The only way we could escape would be . . .

...if SOMEBODY tickled his tail ...

Thank you! Keep on tickling!

Thanks.

OH MY
HEE HEE HO HO
TEE HEE HEE HEE
HA HA
HO HO
TEE
HEE
OH OH
OH

Excuse me
while I go back
to the front of
the book!

Goodbye, Mr. Frimdimpny!

HEE
HEE

SHLOOP
SHLOOP SCOONCH

Bye!

The End